RIPTIDE

R. T. MARTIN

MINNEAPOLIS

Darby Creek
A division of Lerner Publishing Group, Inc.
241 First Avenue North
Minneapolis, MN 55401 USA

For reading levels and more information, look up this title at
www.lernerbooks.com.

Cover and interior images: KIRAYONAK YULIYA/Shutterstock.com (surfer);
XONOVETS/Shutterstock.com (wave texture).

Main body text set in Janson Text LT Std.
Typeface provided by Adobe Systems.

Library of Congress Cataloging-in-Publication Data

Names: Martin, R. T., 1988– author.
Title: Riptide / R. T. Martin.
Description: Minneapolis : Darby Creek, [2019] I Series: To the limit I
    Summary: When a bad storm hits while best friends Maya and Paige are
    surfing, they find themselves trapped on a sandbar, both injured, and with
    a shark nearby.
Identifiers: LCCN 2018019487 (print) I LCCN 2018036304 (ebook) I
    ISBN 9781541541993 (eb pdf) I ISBN 9781541540361 (lb : alk. paper) I
    ISBN 9781541545557 (pb : alk. paper)
Subjects: I CYAC: Surfing—Fiction. I Best friends—Fiction. I
    Friendship—Fiction. I Sharks—Fiction. I Survival—Fiction.
Classification: LCC PZ7.1.M37346 (ebook) I LCC PZ7.1.M37346 Rip 2019 (print) I
    DDC [Fic]—dc23
LC record available at https://lccn.loc.gov/2018019487

Manufactured in the United States of America
1-45241-36623-9/24/2018

For Nate H.

CHAPTER 1

"There's supposed to be a storm today," Paige said.

"Well," Maya replied, "we'll ride until it hits. There's no point staying out of the water because of what will happen later. All in favor say, 'aye.'"

"Aye," Paige said through a laugh. Taking votes between just the two of them had been an inside joke they'd had since they met in the first grade.

They were heading toward the beach with their surfboards tucked under their arms. Dressed in their typical summer uniforms—swimsuits with sneakers they'd take off before they went into the water—and each sporting a small backpack they used to carry their towels, wallets, keys, and cell phones, the girls planned to spend their day like they had almost every other day this summer. Surfing.

Maya could already tell that the shore would be crowded. On the other side of the street, a family was headed the same direction, picnic basket and towels in hand and wearing bathing suits and T-shirts. A few cars passed by that were packed with umbrellas and toys perfect for the beach or a pool. It seemed everyone was trying to soak up as much of this Saturday as possible before the rain started.

There were clouds on the horizon. The storm was just beginning to creep into view, but it was far away, and aside from its looming threat, the conditions for surfing were ideal. The sun was beating down, but the breeze off the water cooled the air to the perfect temperature.

Maya loved surfing more than anything in the world. She'd gone almost every day this summer, many of them like today with her best friend in tow, but summer was coming to a close. Carefree days of riding waves would be replaced with homework and sitting in classrooms. She'd only be able to surf after school, on weekends, and in daydreams for nine months. So she wanted to make the most of what was left of the season.

"Did you get Ms. Kessler for history?" Paige asked. They'd both gotten their class schedules the previous day.

"Can we talk about something other than school?" Maya said. "I'm kind of dreading it. I just want to surf today."

"You want to surf every day." Paige smiled at her.

"Not every day," Maya replied. She was disagreeing just for the sake of it. She *did* want to surf every day, and Paige knew it.

Paige smirked and changed the subject. "How much time do you think we'll have before the storm hits?"

Maya shrugged. "At least a few hours. Hopefully longer."

By now, they weren't far from the beach. Maya could smell the salty breeze coming in from the ocean, and she could hear the waves. Her heart started beating faster, and a smile crept onto her face that she wouldn't have been able to shake even if she had wanted want to. She didn't realize that she'd started walking faster until Paige told her to slow down.

The public beach was crowded with families setting up umbrellas on the sand, and the water was full of people. There were a few surfers here, first-timers mostly, but for Maya and Paige the waves weren't big enough. They were headed to where the *real* surfers went—down the beach where the waves were bigger and where there weren't swimmers getting in the way.

"Slow down!" Paige said again, a little agitated. "The waves aren't going anywhere."

"Sorry," Maya said. "Just excited."

"Be excited at a regular walking pace, please," Paige replied.

Maya nodded to her friend but only slowed down a little as she climbed the large grassy mound that separated the surfing area from the rest of the beach. The mound was about seven feet high and blocked the view of the surfers from the more casual beachgoers. Maya liked that. It made the area feel more private—a special place just for surfers.

She reached the top of the mound and her face fell.

"Great," she said sarcastically.

"What?" Paige asked, just reaching the top of the hill.

Maya didn't answer the question. Paige would see for herself once she looked out at the beach.

"We should have known they'd be here," Paige said flatly.

Kai was standing on the beach next to a cooler gulping down a blue sports drink. As usual, he had about eight friends with him, and they were hogging the surfing area. He tossed the bottle back into the cooler and was just about to grab his board when he saw Maya and Paige standing on the dividing mound. He said something to a couple of the guys he was with and pointed at the girls.

"Maybe we should go somewhere else," Paige suggested.

This wasn't the first time Kai had tried

to keep the surfing area all to himself. Maya wouldn't let it happen today, not on the Saturday before school started.

"Maybe not," she replied quickly. "He doesn't own the ocean or the beach. We can surf where we want." She started down the mound toward the sand, Paige trailing behind her.

Kai undid the strap that attached his board to his ankle and started toward them.

"Nope!" he shouted just as their sneakers hit the sand. "Occupied!" He was waving them back the way they came. "Go somewhere else!" Two of his friends were following close behind him, and the rest of the Kai's group was on high alert. Maya could even see some of his friends in the water sitting on their boards watching to see what would happen.

"You can't tell us what to do, Kai," Maya shouted to him as they got closer.

"We're practicing here," Kai replied. "Our last competition is tomorrow. You two will get in our way."

"There's plenty of water," Paige said. "It's not like—"

"*We're* here," Kai cut her off. "Which means *you* need to go somewhere else."

Maya stepped up so she was just inches from Kai's face. "We'll surf where we want to, and we want to surf here." She crossed her arms. "Why don't you tell me what you're going to do about it?"

Kai scowled. "You know, we actually surf for a *reason*. I won a new board at last week's competition, and the winner this weekend gets five hundred bucks. Surfing is just a hobby for you, so take your hobby back down that way with the rest of the casual boarders."

"If you won your last competition, you should be fine this week," Maya spat back at him.

"I won *because* I practiced," Kai replied.

"You're lucky Maya doesn't compete," Paige said. "If she did, you wouldn't have a shot at that money."

"Is that so?" Kai shot back over Maya's shoulder to Paige.

"Yeah," Maya said firmly. "I've seen you out there, and you're not half as good as you think you are."

Kai looked like he was grinding his teeth. "If you think you're better than me, sign up and prove it."

"Unlike you," Maya said. "I don't need other people to *tell* me I'm good at what I enjoy doing. From where I'm standing, it seems like you only enter competitions because you're an insecure little child. Get out of our way because we're surfing *here*."

Maya had struck a nerve. Kai's eyes narrowed and his face turned red. Even the two friends behind him seemed to sense that Maya had crossed a line.

"You're so much better than me, huh?" Kai's head tilted and an evil smile came over his face. "In that case, why surf here? We'd get in *your* way." His mocking tone made Maya's blood boil. "You should surf where only a pro can pull it off. Why don't you head down to Ripper's Cove?" He looked at each of his friends and nodded to them, prompting them to agree. They both stayed silent and even looked a little concerned at Kai's suggestion.

"Don't be stupid," Paige said at exactly the same moment as Maya shouted "Fine!"

"What?" Paige said, a little dumbfounded.

"Great!" Kai said, still smirking. "We'll be here practicing, and you'll be at Ripper's Cove proving how good you are. Sounds perfect to me."

"Sounds good to me too," Maya said. She knew she was rising to Kai's bait, but she didn't care. "I'm happy to shred up some waves you're too scared to touch."

Kai eyes narrowed again, but he smiled through it. "Great. Have fun."

CHAPTER 2

"Okay," Paige said once they were out of earshot of Kai and his friends. "So where are we actually going?" They were walking down the boardwalk that lined the beach.

"Ripper's Cove," Maya said flatly.

"You're not serious." Paige stared hard at Maya, who was avoiding eye contact.

"I *am* serious. He thinks he's better than us, so let's prove he's not by surfing somewhere he's too afraid to go."

"This is stupid. Like, *really* stupid." Paige groaned. "There's a good reason he's afraid to go there."

"Yeah," Maya said. "He's not good enough."

"I'm kind of thinking it has more to do with the sharp, dangerous rocks everywhere," Paige replied.

"We'll be fine." Maya was walking fast again, but this time it was out of anger, not excitement. "We're both better surfers than he is. We can surf Ripper's Cove, no problem. As long as we're careful, neither of us will get hurt."

Ripper's Cove was actually named Ripley's Cove, at least that's what it was called on every map of the area. But none of the locals ever called it by its real name. The cove was about a mile down the beach from where Kai and his friends were surfing, and no one would be there. No one was ever there. It was too dangerous. Unlike where Kai was practicing, the ocean floor at Ripper's Cove was mostly sharp, jagged rock rather than soft sand. Everyone in town called it Ripper's Cove because anyone who surfed there was pretty likely to get shredded by the rocks, at least according to the legend. Maya had never actually surfed there herself.

"Megan Wolf broke her arm there last year," Paige said. She was more or less pleading with Maya to turn back. "Mike Franssen slashed open his leg! He had to get thirty-seven stitches!"

"Megan and Mike are amateurs," Maya said, waving away Paige's concern. "They're not even as good as Kai, and we're *both* better than he is."

"Maybe you are, but—"

"We'll be *fine*. Besides, they weren't careful. They went to Ripper's Cove just for bragging rights—to say they did it."

"Uhh," Paige said. "Isn't that kind of what we're doing?"

"No!" Maya said a little too defensively. "We're . . . making the most of summer." Even she had to admit her argument was pretty thin. "We're going to Ripper's Cove. All in favor say 'aye.'"

Paige rolled her eyes. "Nay! Let's just go somewhere else. There are a dozen places to surf around here. It's not like Kai's going to check. Let's *not* surf there and say we did."

"Paige," Maya said, turning around to face her friend. "We'll be fine. As long as we're careful and we head out beyond the rocks, we'll be perfectly safe. Besides, if anything happens to one of us, the other one will be there to help."

"Yeah," Paige admitted. "That's true."

Maya nodded, satisfied with the answer and turned around to keep walking.

"Will you stop walking so fast?" Paige said, softer this time than before.

"Yeah," Maya said, slowing down. "Sorry, I'm just . . . I'm just mad."

"Don't let Kai get to you."

Maya didn't say anything. She just kept walking, although now she made more of an effort to walk at a reasonable pace.

Kai had been like this for years. Even Maya had to admit that he'd earned the right to be proud of his skills. Back when they were ten years old, Kai had entered a competition that was supposed to be for ages twelve to fifteen and won the thing. He nearly got the trophy too, but one of the kids he'd just barely edged out tattled on him to the judges. He'd been disqualified, unable to go home with the trophy that was nearly as tall as he was, but that hadn't stopped his ego from inflating.

Even though Paige didn't think of herself as the strongest surfer, Maya knew she was still good enough not to injure herself on the rocks. Kai might be afraid of Ripper's Cove, but Maya wasn't. *And there's no reason Paige should be either*, she thought.

"Did you hear about those two windsurfers?" Paige said. She was obviously trying to steer the conversation away from Kai.

"Huh?" Maya said. She hadn't been paying attention.

"Those two windsurfers. Just a couple days ago." Paige said again.

"No. What happened? They get hurt?"

"One of them, yeah," Paige said, a little concern in her voice. "Shark."

"Seriously?" Maya stopped for a second.

"Yup," Paige replied. "Apparently it came out of nowhere."

"Are they all right?" Maya had heard of only a few shark attacks around the area, and most of them had been minor—smaller sharks that couldn't do any real damage. They'd bite someone and freak out everyone at the beach, but the real danger was minimal.

"One of them is fine," Paige said. "But the other one is still in the hospital. Apparently he got his board snapped in half and his leg chewed up pretty badly. I heard the shark was huge."

"What kind of shark was it?"

Paige got a serious look on her face. "Bull shark."

Maya felt a shiver go down her spine. Movies and TV shows with scary shark scenes always show a great white because they're so big. But most suffers know great whites prefer open water, so they don't usually come around the shore. Bull sharks are something else entirely. They are only about a third as big but five times meaner. Their smaller size allows them to come closer to shore just to rip and thrash at anything unfortunate enough to be in the water at the time.

Bull sharks terrified Maya.

Her uncle had accidentally hooked one while fishing just off the coast once. It had been strong enough to pull him straight out of the boat by the fishing pole. Luckily he'd managed to make it back onto the boat before the shark could attack. "I lost a pole, but I kept my life," he said when he told the story to Maya's family. "Pure luck that I'm alive."

"They're lucky," Maya said about the two windsurfers.

"Yeah," Paige replied. "That's what they said too."

Maya felt another shiver. "I changed my mind. Let's talk about school."

Paige laughed. The girls chatted about their schedules for the upcoming year. Paige had already committed hers to memory: times, teachers, classroom numbers. Maya barely remembered what classes she was taking. But from what Paige was telling her, it sounded like they were going to have at least a few classes together this year.

It took a little over twenty minutes of walking for the two friends to reach Ripper's Cove. There was no formal entrance to the cove, so they had to hop the wooden fence of the boardwalk, cross some grass, and walk down an embankment just to get there.

Even the beach of the cove wasn't particularly inviting. Most of the sand was covered by long, flat pieces of shale rock. With their shoes on, they'd be fine, but once they took them off, they'd have to pay attention to where they stepped. The edges of the rocks were razor sharp. But the serious danger was when they were in the water. Maya knew that larger pieces of the same sharp shale were hidden under the waves. And they might be tilted at angles, ready to impale whatever fell on them. For a second, she wanted to scrap the plan—turn around and either surf somewhere else or even *do* something else.

No, she thought, pushing the thought from

her brain. *It's the last weekend of surfing. We came all the way here. We're doing this.*

She walked confidently onto the beach, past the sign that read:

RIPLEY'S COVE

ROCKY AREA.
SURFING NOT ADVISED.
ENTER WATER AT
YOUR OWN RISK.

CHAPTER 3

"At least the waves are perfect," Paige said as they walked to the edge of the shore, the shale rock sliding beneath their feet. The waves were huge, rolling toward shore and curling in on themselves, absolutely ideal for surfing. If it wasn't for all the sharp rocks, there wasn't a doubt in Maya's mind that people would be surfing here all day, every day.

The storm clouds were still covering the horizon, but the darkest of them were still a long way off. The girls would have plenty of time to ride waves before it started raining or the waves became too unpredictable.

Maya eyed the waves, trying to decide the

safest way for them to surf the cove. "Here's what I'm thinking: we paddle out a little farther than we usually do, and then once we're surfing, we'll bail out before the water's shallow enough for us to hit the bottom."

"How do we know where that is?"

"We'll do a few spot checks on our way out."

Paige tilted her head. "It actually doesn't look so bad. Yeah. You're right. I think we'll be fine." She smiled at Maya. "Let's make the most of summer. All in favor say 'aye.'"

"Aye," Maya said, smiling from ear to ear.

They both took off their shoes and pulled their towels out of their bags before dropping their backpacks next to their shoes. They each put their towel next to the backpacks and set out toward the water.

Maya was extra careful walking barefoot to the water's edge. The last thing she wanted to do was cut open her foot before getting into the water. Slowly, she and Paige made their way down the beach to where the waves washed up on the shore.

With the water splashing over their feet,

they attached their ankle leashes, four-foot bungee cords that made sure they would always be attached to their boards. Maya undid and reattached her ankle strap three times, making sure it would stay strong when she bailed out early on the waves.

They got in the water and started paddling out.

"Check it out," Paige shouted to Maya over the crashing waves. She nodded to something off to Maya's left, a sand bar pretty far out from the beach itself, a narrow little strip of dry land that pointed out to sea like an arrow. "If something goes wrong and we can't make it to shore, let's head there."

"Good plan," Maya shouted back.

They headed out about as far as they would normally go before Maya did the first spot check to see how shallow the water was. She dove under and felt around gently with her hands. It was about seven, maybe eight feet down before she hit the rocks. "We've got to head farther out," she said when she came back up. "Too shallow here."

Paige nodded, and they continued paddling into deeper water, diving under the waves as they rolled in.

Maya did three more spot checks. On the third, the water seemed to be nearly fifteen feet deep. It was perfect. If they bailed here, there was virtually no chance they'd risk hitting the rocky bottom.

"This is it," she said when she popped out from the water and back onto her board. "We should be safe if we bail here."

They continued paddling out to sea. The waves were getting bigger the farther they got from shore. Their size only excited Maya. *The bigger the wave, the faster the ride*, she thought.

Eventually, when she thought they could have a nice ride before bailing at the safe spot, Maya turned her board back toward the shore. She hopped on the next wave that came rolling by.

This was what she loved. Riding a board along a wave, she felt almost weightless but in perfect control. She could go faster than she ever could on foot, and it was impossible for her to have any care in the world. The dread of the new school year, Kai's obnoxious behavior, it all faded out of her mind. All she cared about was the wave and her board. *And the rocks*, Maya reminder herself. She had to care about them. She kept a close eye on the spot where she knew it was safest to bail off the board.

When she reached the spot, she kicked the board out from under her, flicking it forward while she herself jumped backward over the crest of the wave. She hit the water and felt the ankle leash go taut for a second. Then it loosened as the bungee cord snapped it back toward her body. Maya resurfaced. She hadn't hit a rock. She hadn't hit anything. This was actually turning out to be safer than she'd expected. She made her way to her board, which was floating just a few feet away.

Maya wrapped an arm over her board, swooped a leg across it and swiftly pulled herself back on top of it. Paige was still waiting, obviously making sure Maya was okay before she took a ride herself. Maya gave her a big thumbs-up, and Paige grinned back. Maya watched as Paige waited for a wave and hopped onto her board.

Paige jumped off further out than Maya had. *She's probably still a little nervous*, Maya thought as she waited for her friend to resurface. When Paige did pop up from the water, she had a big smile on her face.

"Let's rip this cove up!" she shouted.

Maya just laughed and started paddling out again.

They each caught another wave. Then another. Maya was a little surprised at how easy surfing this area really was. *The people who got injured must have been really careless*, Maya thought. As long as they bailed out before the wave got too close to the shore, there was virtually no danger that they'd get hurt.

Each time Maya jumped off her board and popped her head above water, she was reminded of the storm. They sky was getting darker and grayer with each passing moment. Not only that, but the waves were also growing less manageable, and the wind was starting to pick up.

After Paige caught a particularly big wave, she resurfaced and called out to Maya. "Maybe we should think about heading back."

Maya looked at the sky. "We came all the way out here. We should make the most of it!" She had to shout the last bit so that Paige would hear her over the waves crashing nearby.

Paige seemed a little hesitant about continuing but shrugged and started paddling back out.

They surfed for another half hour. Maya had just started riding a massive wave when it swelled, becoming much larger than she anticipated. The wind whipped into a frenzy, and she nearly lost her balance as she rode toward shore. She corrected her footing, and then leaned into the wind and angled the board a little bit, steadying herself. This wave was moving faster than the previous ones. It only took about half the usual time for her to reach the point where it was still safe to jump off, and she nearly missed it, getting too close to the dangerous rocks beneath. When she came back to the surface, she looked for Paige.

It was definitely time to head back to shore. The conditions were becoming treacherous.

Paige was out where they were catching the waves, just about to ride an approaching swell. *Perfect*, Maya thought. *After this one, we should both head in.* The storm was picking up in a hurry, and by the time Maya made it back to where they were catching the waves, the water would be too choppy to ride anyway.

Paige jumped up on her board, riding the surf in. She wasn't far from Maya when the wave swelled and crashed in on itself without warning. Just before Maya pushed her board down to swim under the wave she saw Paige disappear into the crashing water. When she popped her head out of the water, Paige was nowhere to be seen. Maya couldn't even spot Paige's board. It was as if she'd vanished into the ocean.

Much farther out from shore than she expected, there was a splash, and she heard Paige's voice call, "He—" It cut off. "Help!"

Maya paddled toward Paige, ducking under the waves as she went and fighting the water pushing against her. The storm was coming into full effect now. Not only were there waves washing in toward the shore, but the wind was whipping water down the coast. Maya was getting splashed from the side as she made her way to Paige.

Paige would appear for a moment, only to disappear behind a swell. Maya knew she was moving in generally the right direction, but she kept losing sight of her friend.

We stayed too long, she thought. They'd missed their window to make it back to shore by mere minutes, and now Paige needed help. Maya tried to reassure herself that her friend was probably fine—fighting a pulled muscle or dealing with a cracked board.

But then Maya heard something that cut through the noise of the waves. Paige was crying.

CHAPTER 4

"My left leg!" Paige shouted when Maya eventually swam up to her. Paige was bobbing up and down in the waves, clinging to the side of her board. "I think it's broken!" The sound of crashing waves nearly drowned her out voice entirely.

"Can you make it to shore?" Maya asked, steadying Paige's board, afraid it might tip over, dumping her friend into to ocean.

Paige glanced toward the shore, winced in pain, and shook her head. "Sandbar!" she shouted.

Maya looked around for the sandbar. The storm was making the water so chaotic that it was hard to see *anything*, much less the narrow sandbar they'd agreed to meet at if they couldn't make it to shore.

"That way!" Paige shouted, seeing that Maya couldn't tell where it was.

"You need to get on your board!" Maya yelled. "Once you're on, grab my hand, and I'll paddle and pull you."

Paige winced in pain again. She took a deep breath and hoisted herself onto the board. She swung her right leg out of the water, screaming as she did so. Then she shook her head. "I can't get the other one up. It's definitely broken."

Maya gripped Paige's hand tightly as Paige used her other one to grip her own board. Using her free hand, Maya started paddling in the direction Paige had pointed. She still couldn't see exactly where they were going, so she just had to trust her friend.

Maya considered just heading toward shore but thought better of it. Yes, their phones were there, and she could call someone for help, but she didn't think they could make it past the rocks. It would be hard enough getting herself on shore, and Maya knew that she would have the advantage of being able to walk onto the beach from the shallow water. Paige wasn't so lucky. And with the waves coming in faster and stronger with the storm, the likelihood of getting knocked off their boards and hitting the rocks in the shallow water was even higher. The sandbar was definitely a better and safer option. If only Maya could find it.

Between the waves and the unpredictable current of the storm, Maya couldn't be sure how far they'd gone or if they were even headed in the right direction. She just kept paddling the way Paige had pointed and hoped they would hit the sandbar soon . . . although she had no idea what they'd do once they were there.

The storm was getting worse by the second. Swells of waves continued washing up over the edge of Maya's board into her face. Every few strokes, she was splashed with salty sea water. She spit the water out just to get splashed again, but she wouldn't stop. Paige needed her to keep going.

For nearly ten minutes, Maya paddled while pulling Paige along with her. Every second, she felt more and more hopeless. Even though she couldn't see it, she also couldn't help thinking the strip of dry land was getting farther and farther away.

Just when Maya had the desperate thought that they weren't going to make it, the sandbar came into view. They were close—a lot closer than Maya thought they'd be.

"I can see it!" she shouted to Paige over the thrashing ocean.

Paige didn't respond, and for a second, Maya thought she might have passed out, but then her friend squeezed her hand a little tighter. Maya let out a sigh of relief and continued paddling.

Land. Although the sandbar was narrow, Maya felt her foot graze the ocean floor about ten feet out from it. For the first time ever, Maya was relieved to be able to get out of the water. She jumped off her board, and the water only reached about halfway up her shin. Maya gripped the front of Paige's board and started pulling it toward safety. She dragged it, with Paige aboard, out of the water and onto the sand.

Sometime during the paddling, Paige had managed to get her broken leg onto the board. And it was *definitely* broken. Halfway down the shin, it was bent at a strange and extremely unnatural angle. She also had a large gash up most of her leg. It wasn't bleeding much, but it looked deep . . . and painful.

Looking at Paige's bent leg, Maya had to resist the urge to throw up. But she pushed the feeling aside. Paige needed her.

Paige was grimacing in pain on the sand. Maya saw she'd bitten her lip hard enough for it to bleed. Maya pulled Paige and her board up the sandbar, farther from the waves lapping up around them.

"Is it bad?" Paige struggled to sit up and look at her leg. The pain was too much, and she laid back down with a groan.

Maya was about to say *No, not at all*, but she knew Paige wouldn't believe it. "It's not good," she said instead.

"Is it broken?"

"Yeah." Maya was panicking but desperately trying not to show it. She'd never seen someone's leg bent like this. It was like something out of a horror movie. She had no idea how to reset a broken leg. She desperately wanted to help, but Paige's injuries were much more severe than anything Maya could fix. The best thing she could do was keep her friend as warm and dry as possible.

"What happened?" Maya asked.

"The current," Paige replied through a wince. "It pushed me down. I tried to turn in the water, but my leg hit a rock hard."

She leaned up on her board and looked at her own leg. "I need to go to the hospital!" she shouted over the crashing waves.

Maya snapped out of her daze of confusion and panic. She looked toward shore.

There were a hundred, maybe a hundred and fifty yards of angry ocean between her and the rocky beach where their phones were. The sand bar was protected, and the water around it relatively calm, but that calm only spread about ten yards beyond the bar itself. She wouldn't be able to make it very far out before it would be rough going.

"I'm going to go for it!" Maya yelled to Paige.

"Are you insane?"

"I have to! You said it yourself, you need a doctor!"

"You'll get ripped apart on the rocks!" Paige shouted. That was exactly what Maya had been afraid of. Paddling to the shore from this distance during a storm could be dangerous on a regular beach. At Ripper's Cove, it was practically a death wish. "We should wait it—"

Suddenly, big heavy raindrops started falling. They grew thicker and heavier in a matter of seconds, like someone had flipped a switch. Maya saw Paige fight back a scream. The hard rain must have felt like hammers hitting her broken leg.

She didn't have a choice. Without waiting for Paige to continue whatever she had been saying, Maya grabbed her board and dove into the raging ocean.

CHAPTER 5

Maya could hear Paige calling to her from the sandbar, but her voice was drowned out by the crashing of waves and the sound of rain. Maya kept paddling. If she could just make it to shore, she could grab her phone and call 911.

The rain pounding down was cold, and Maya wished she'd worn her wetsuit. It would have provided at least a little insulation. Her thin summer swimsuit wasn't meant for this kind of weather. She shivered even as she worked hard to move herself toward the beach. Maya knew that in conditions like this, hypothermia was a real possibility.

And the trip wasn't easy. Making it from where Paige broke her leg to the sandbar had been difficult, but trying to navigate the raging waters during the storm was close to impossible. Unlike the predictable waves of the afternoon, the storm was pushing water in all different directions. Larger waves were coming from behind her, but smaller ones were pushing her to either side or splashing up over the front of her board. She was constantly choking on water that flew into her mouth and trying to correct the angle of her board so that she was headed toward shore and not down the coast.

After nearly ten minutes of fighting the waves, she looked back to see how far she'd gotten. Paige had somehow slipped off her board and was now hiding under it, protecting herself from the rain. Maya could see her clearly, and the shore didn't seem to be any closer than when she'd started. She'd only made it maybe twenty or thirty yards at the most.

Maya had the horrible thought that no matter how hard she fought the waves and the rain, there might be no possible way for her to make it to the shore.

And then a bright flash of lightning lit up the sky, followed by rolling thunder that sounded like it started far away but grew to the level of an explosion. Literally everyone knew to stay out of the water whenever there was lightning. A nearby bolt could shock Maya, knocking her out, and then she'd drown.

Maya pushed even harder to make it to shore. But the longer she did, the less likely it seemed that she'd actually make it. All the odds were stacked against her. The waves, the lightning . . . even the rain had become so heavy the shore looked hazy, and it was possible that she would lose sight of it, not to mention the sandbar.

That's when it happened. A wave slammed into her side, flipping her off her board. As soon as she entered the water, Maya felt the current pull her down.

Within seconds, she lost her bearings— unable to figure out which way was up in the surging water.

Wham. Maya's head slammed against a rock on the ocean floor. Her vision flashed and her ears started ringing. The pain made her gasp, and water filled her lungs. She was drowning. Her mind screamed at her, *Get to the surface!*

She pivoted in the water and pushed off the same rock she'd hit her head on, but the current shoved her sideways, and she lost her bearings again. Her body wanted to choke, spit up the water she inhaled and take a breath, but she fought the impulse. If she choked now, she'd just swallow more water.

Just when there seemed like no way out, a thought flashed across Maya's waterlogged mind. *My board. It would float to the surface.* She grabbed hold of her ankle leash and followed it. It *had* to be the way up.

She made her way through the dark water with the leash as her guide and came up directly under her board. As soon as she made it to the surface, Maya heaved up the water she'd breathed in. Just as she did, a wave rolled over her head, filling her mouth and lungs with more water.

She grabbed the edge of her board and climbed on top of it, choking again and desperately gasping for air. Her head was throbbing, radiating pain from the place it had made contact with the rocks. She gently put a hand to it. There didn't seem to be a cut, but if there was, it was so small she couldn't feel it.

Maya tried to find Paige and the sandbar amidst the waves. It took her a moment, but her friend was still there, her board still covering her, a poor excuse for a tent. In the time Maya had spent getting thrown off the board and sloshed around underwater, she'd ended up closer to the sandbar than she'd been when she fell off. All that work for nothing except hitting her head and nearly drowning.

Paige had been right. There was no way Maya would be able to make it to shore. She hadn't even made it to the part of the coast that really scared her, the sharp jagged rocks right by the beach.

Maya turned the board back toward the sandbar and started paddling for it. She made it there in half the time it had taken her to paddle the same distance away.

As Maya pulled her board up onto shore and used it to block some of the rain, Paige poked her head out from underneath her own board.

"I told you that was a bad idea! I lost sight of you. How far did you make it?"

"Not far." Maya lay down on the wet sand next to Paige and covered herself with the board just as her friend was doing. It wasn't much, but it did block some of the rain. Maya tried to look out across the water, but staring at the waves made her dizzy. When she sat up to get a better look, she realized the dizziness wasn't just from the water, but rather the splitting pain coming from her head. Every move she made, her head ached and she felt slightly nauseous. Maya may not have cut her head open, but she seemed to have hit it hard enough for it to have left a lasting effect.

"We need to get to shore!" Shouting made her head throb. But Maya knew that Paige must be in more pain than she was.

Paige shook her head. "That's not going to happen during the storm. We just have to wait it out!"

"If I can just make it to our phones . . ." Maya trailed off.

"What made you turn back?" Paige asked, still yelling over the thunderous sound of rain hitting the boards.

"What?"

"Why did you turn back?" Paige said slower and louder.

"I got knocked off," Maya replied.

Paige shook her head and winced in pain again. "If you try to go out again and don't make it to shore, it makes the situation a thousand times worse. I won't be the only one who needs medical attention." She looked out at the waves toward the shore. "We have to wait it out."

Maya didn't like it, but Paige was right. *I nearly died out there once*, she thought. *And this storm is just getting worse. But it has to let up soon.*

As if nature were trying to prove her wrong,

lightning flashed again, followed by the thunder that sounded more like a train running them over. A gust of wind swept past that was so strong it nearly sent their boards sailing out of their hands.

The storm was not letting up. In fact, it was only getting worse.

CHAPTER 6

The sky was so dark it might as well have been nighttime. The only light was from the constant lightning flashes that made Maya think of a broken strobe light—uneven and random bursts of bright in the dark. The rain was heavy and only getting heavier. The surfboards were doing next to nothing in the way of protecting the two girls. The wind was pushing the rain at different angles each moment. First it would pound on their right sides, then the wind would shift, and their left sides would get soaked.

Maya stood up, fighting against her dizziness and the beating rain, to try and arrange the boards in a way that might keep them a little drier. First, she tried to prop them into the sand at an angle so they would be a little more like a tent, but the wind blew the two boards straight out of the ground. If they hadn't had their ankle leashes still attached, they would have lost the boards forever. The fact that Paige's leash was attached to her right leg was an unforeseen blessing. Maya shuddered as she thought about how painful it would have been for her friend's broken left leg to be jerked in the direction of the flying board.

She tried a few other ways of arranging the boards, but the result was always that they either flew away or provided little shelter. In the end, they both decided the most practical thing was just to lie on their backs holding the boards over their bodies. At least that way, they could be sure they wouldn't lose their only means of getting back to shore.

It wasn't just the rain that was a problem. Some of the waves were big enough to wash over the sandbar. Every few minutes, they'd get slammed with a wall of water, not big enough to push them into the ocean but definitely big enough to cause Paige significant pain. Maya saw Paige clench her jaw and slam her eyes shut every time it happened. She'd breathe deeply for a few moments, but when she noticed Maya looking, she did her best to look like she was perfectly fine. It was obvious she wasn't.

The minutes dragged on. The intense pain in Maya's head was becoming more of a dull ache, but Maya became more and more concerned for her friend. Paige was turning pale.

"Maybe we can make a splint or something," Maya suggested.

"Out of what?" Paige asked through clenched teeth.

"My board. I'll break it apart if it'll help."

"Maybe if I'd just sprained it, but you saw it. The bone needs to be reset. Do you know how to do that?"

Maya shook her head.

"Then I'd rather you didn't touch it," Paige said flatly.

Helplessness washed over Maya. The feeling reminded her of the fourth grade. There had been a class hamster, Scoots. Each kid got to take Scoots home for a weekend to care for and play with the little guy. During the weekend he spent at Maya's house, she got home from surfing with her parents on Saturday and went into her room to feed the hamster. He was just lying there, breathing but not moving. She put food in his dish, but the hamster didn't seem to care. All of Sunday, she sat at her desk with her chin on her hands watching the tiny animal in its cage. Scoots didn't move. He didn't eat. He didn't drink water.

There was a part of Maya that knew what was happening, even if she didn't want to accept it. She'd felt embarrassed and ashamed then—the same way she felt now on the sandbar. She was unable to help, paralyzed by circumstances beyond her control, forced to just wait for the outcome.

On Monday, after that weekend in fourth grade, Maya had brought Scoots' cage back to the teacher, but the hamster wasn't in it. Maya tried to shake the memory. *Paige is going to be fine*, she told herself. But even as she did, Maya wasn't sure she believed it.

"I'm going to try again," Maya said.

"Try what again?"

"I'm going to try for the shore."

"Are you out of your mind?" Paige sounded equally confused and angry. "The storm's gotten ten times worse! There's no way you'll make it!"

"You need help, and this thing isn't letting up!"

Paige grabbed her hand. "You're not going out there! I don't care if I have to tackle you, broken leg or not! You're not doing it!" She paused for a second, then gave Maya a sad little smile. "All in favor say 'aye!'" she shouted over the rain and ocean.

Maya shook her head and started grinding her teeth, but she stayed put. "Aye."

The storm seemed to have reached its peak. It was bad, but at least it wasn't getting any worse. *Anything worse would be a hurricane*, Maya thought. She kept one hand holding her board in place and rhythmically pounded the other one on the sand. The pounding gave her something to focus on other than the

lightning, the rain, and her friend's broken leg.
There wasn't anything she could do, at least
not right now.

Another flash of lightning lit up the dark
water in front of them. Maya thought she saw
something. The strobe effect of the storm
made it hard to see clearly, but for just a second,
she was sure it was there. It was floating farther
out, somewhere between the sandbar and the
coast, and even the briefest sight of it made
Maya's skin crawl and gave her the sensation of
a centipede crawling up and down her spine.

She could have sworn she saw a shark's fin
cutting through the top of a wave.

CHAPTER 7

Maya spent the next twenty minutes scanning the water with each flash of lightning. The sloshing water and the rain made the task difficult. Everything was hazy at best, but she focused hard on the water in front of her. After maybe two dozen more flashes, she hadn't caught sight of it again.

A part of her wanted to tell Paige what she'd seen. But Paige was looking worse and worse. Not only was she pale, but her lips were definitely blue now. She looked sick—like she had pretty bad case of the flu—and her eyes were fluttering as if she were actively trying to keep them from closing. The last thing she needed was to find out there might be a shark in the water. Besides, Maya had only seen it for a brief second. She didn't want to worry her friend over nothing.

She stared hard, scanning the water to the best of her ability, but Maya didn't see the fin again. She remembered what Paige had told her on their way to Ripper's Cove—the news about the windsurfer who'd been attacked by a bull shark not long ago.

I'm just imagining things, she told herself. The idea of a shark was planted in her mind, and now she was just projecting the image onto something harmless in the water. *I saw driftwood or some kid's arm floatie. Nature wouldn't be cruel enough to make this situation worse.* She almost believed herself, but she continued to scan the water for the fin. Sooner or later, they were going to have to make their way across the waves and onto land. She wanted to be as sure as possible that there wasn't a dangerous predator blocking their path.

It took what felt like at least an hour, but

eventually the lightning flashes became less frequent. The rain began to get lighter, the sky turned from almost pitch black to a deep gray, and the wind began to die down.

"Okay, I think it's safe," Maya said. "I'm going to go for it."

Paige didn't respond.

"Paige?" Maya said, looking to her friend. Paige was unconscious, lying motionless beneath the surfboard. "Paige!" Maya shouted, shaking her gently. Paige didn't wake up. Sometime during the storm, she must have passed out from pain or exhaustion. Either way, Maya needed to get her medical attention as soon as possible. Maya ran into the water, jumped on her board, and began paddling as fast as she could. Normally, she would have surfed into the shore, but this was no time to take unnecessary risks. She was far past the point where she and Paige had agreed to bail off their boards for fear of hitting the rocks below. She'd paddle until she could run.

It wasn't easy. Her head felt as though it was full of cotton and the water wasn't helping much either. There were still some swells and waves that Maya didn't anticipate. They threatened to push her off the board, or at the very least, farther down the coast.

Just get to the phone. Just get to the phone. Just get to the phone, she kept repeating in her mind. Her heart was racing, and she was tired and cold, but she could deal with all that later—after she got Paige the help she needed.

Maya paddled harder than she had ever done in her life. As soon as she got close enough that she could touch the bottom, she got up, picked up her board, and sprinted to where she saw their bags. The towels were gone, and one of Paige's shoes had vanished, having blown away in the storm, but the bags had miraculously stayed put.

Kneeling down, she undid her ankle leash and dug in her bag to get her phone. She tried to unlock her phone, but nothing happened. The screen stayed dark. *Maybe it turned off*, she desperately hoped. She held down on the power button, but still, nothing happened.

"No, no, no, no, no!" she shouted out loud

without meaning to. *It must have gotten too wet in the rain!*

She tossed it back into her bag and began digging in Paige's bag for her phone. She hit the power button, but just like with the first phone, nothing happened.

Maya didn't know whether she wanted to scream or cry. Maybe both. She took a few deep breaths to force her mind to slow down. Home. Her parents. It would take nearly thirty minutes, but her parents should be there. They could call an ambulance, the Coast Guard, someone. Maya didn't like the idea of leaving Paige out there alone, but there weren't any other options at this point.

Maya looked at her friend lying on the sandbar. She felt like she was forgetting something, some pivotal danger that she hadn't accounted for. There was some reason she couldn't leave her friend lying there while she ran for help.

The tide! Maya's mind screamed.

It would come in soon, which meant the water level near shore would be rising. It was approaching late afternoon, and within a couple of hours, the sandbar would be completely underwater. Even if Paige wasn't already unconscious, she had a badly broken leg. She wouldn't be able to tread water very well, much less swim to shore.

Every muscle in Maya's body ached, but she gritted her teeth, strapped the ankle leash back on, and headed toward the water. She had to bring Paige back to shore. *As painful as this will be for me, it's going to be worse for Paige*, she told herself as she ran back out into the waves.

She got on the board and started paddling. Her body wanted so badly to rest, but she continued.

She caught a glimpse of something out of the corner of her eye. It was about forty feet from her. It sliced through the water briefly before dipping under again.

Maya felt her heart skip a beat as she remembered the fin she thought she saw during the storm. She sat up on her board and stayed perfectly still. Maybe it was just her mind playing tricks on her again. There wasn't anything there, just driftwood.

A seagull landed on the water and started cleaning its wing with its beak right where Maya thought she had seen the shark. She stared at it hard.

The bull shark leaped out of the water and attacked the bird so quickly that Maya flinched and fell off her board and into the water. When she resurfaced, the bird was gone, but a single feather was floating on the water where it had been.

Maya scrambled back on her board so quickly she surprised even herself. Back above the water and safely on her surfboard, she turned and started paddling as fast as she could back to the shore. The second she could run, she did, sprinting like her life depended on it—back onto the rocks of Ripper's Cove, back onto dry land where that creature couldn't get her.

She'd only seen it for a second, but she saw it clearly. Not only was it a bull shark, it was a full-grown adult—much bigger than even the ones at the zoo. Maya tried to control her breathing. Adrenaline was pumping through her body, and she realized she was shaking.

Just then, the shark's dorsal fin appeared again. It cut through the water halfway between the coast and the sandbar. It was patrolling the waters between Maya and the spot where Paige lay helplessly on the ever-shrinking sandbar.

CHAPTER 8

Going back in the water wasn't an option.
Maya undid her ankle leash and put her shoes
on. They were soaking wet, but that didn't
matter. She just needed something on her feet
as she ran.

It was going to be a long run, and she had
to make it fast. She slipped twice just trying to
get off the beach of Ripper's Cove. The shale
rocks were slick with rain and slid out from
under her feet. She picked herself up each time,
and even though her hands hurt from each fall,
she didn't bother to check for injuries. There
simply wasn't time.

She bolted down the cove's rocky beach,

feeling especially unsteady, and up the hill onto the boardwalk. Running on the boardwalk was easier, but Maya still felt sluggish. She didn't know exactly how long she had before Paige would be underwater. *Shark infested water*, Maya thought. As if it wasn't bad enough that Paige might drown, the shark swimming around the sandbar would be sure to go for the easy, injured prey.

Maya started pumping her legs a little faster, fighting against her body's urge to slow down. There was absolutely no way she was going to let anything else happen to Paige. She needed to make it home. Her parents could help, call the police or an ambulance, maybe the Coast Guard. They needed to get *someone* out to Ripper's Cove and fast.

She reached the beach where they'd intended to surf. Maya's legs were burning from the effort. Her quads felt like they were going numb, and she was sure she'd have blisters on her feet for the next few days. *Can't stop*, she thought. *Push through it. Push through it.*

She passed the dividing mound between the surfing part of the beach and the casual area, ran for another block, and hung a left toward the residential neighborhood. Still a couple of miles to go.

Her chest hurt from heavy breathing, and even though she was cold and wet, she could feel beads of sweat running down her back.

Just then she realized her parents might not be home. It was Saturday, and sometimes they went out to dinner on the weekends. But she didn't stop. *I'll have to go to the neighbors*, she thought, her feet pounding beneath her.

"You trying to ditch your friend?"

Maya snapped her head to the side. Kai was sitting on the front porch of his house with his feet up on the wooden railing.

Maya took a sharp turn. Instead of continuing down the street, she ran right up to Kai's porch. For a second he looked nervous. He probably thought that Maya was coming to confront him . . . or worse.

"Give me your phone," she said, trying to catch her breath.

"No," he replied, looking confused.

"Give me your phone!" she cried louder and angrier.

"No!" he shouted back. "Use your own!"

"It's broken! Give me yours!"

"Not if you broke your *own* phone. These things cost money, you know," he said, holding up his cell phone and wiggling it in the air.

"I need it! Paige is—" Maya was trying to catch her breath and fight the pounding in her head. She swayed. Her vision was blurry, and she felt like she was about to pass out. "Paige is—" She tried to steady herself on the porch railing.

"Paige is what? Spit it out!"

Maya was struck by a wave of nausea that seemed to radiate directly from the place where she had hit her head.

"Paige is in trouble! Trapped. Leg. Broken. Sandbar. Shark." She was only able to spit out key words, but it she still managed to get Kai's attention.

"Wait, what? Shark?"

"She broke—" Paige gripped the railing

even tighter. "Her Leg. Stuck on a sandbar at—" She blinked hard, trying to steady her vision. "Ripper's Cove. Tide's coming in. There's—" Deep breath. "A shark. Bull shark. In the water. I can't get to her." The world was no longer spinning, but Maya kept a hold on the railing just in case. "So give me your phone!"

Kai's eyes went wide, and he quickly handed it over.

Maya dialed 911 and put it to her ear.

"We're sorry," a recorded voice on the other side of the line said. "All available operators are currently busy. Stay on the line and we will be with you as soon as possible."

Maya hung up and dialed again.

"We're sorry."

She hung up and dialed a third time.

"We're sorry."

She nearly threw Kai's phone into the street before she stopped herself. "It's busy!" she said. "How is that possible?"

Kai's mouth pulled to one side. "It's probably because of the wreck."

"What?"

"The wreck. Haven't you seen the news?"

"No! I haven't seen the news, Kai!"

"Right." He looked a little embarrassed. "A ship crashed into the dock over by Pier Eight during the storm. Power's out in a lot of places, and there was a big fire. The emergency lines are probably swamped."

Maya felt a whole new wave of nausea that didn't seem to be coming from the pain in her head. "What about the Coast Guard?"

"They were called to help out emergency services." He pointed past the beach where people enjoyed the sun and sand to the docks. "You can see it from here."

Sure enough, Maya saw a big cloud of black smoke rising from a mile or two away. Maya felt her heart race as she wondered if she'd ever see Paige again.

"She's at Ripper's Cove, right?" Kai asked.

Maya nodded. "Stuck on a sandbar."

"If I can distract the shark, can you make it to Paige?"

Maya turned to him. She was about ready to

collapse, but she could keep fighting through it if it meant saving her friend. "Yeah, but how are you going to distract the shark?"

The corners of Kai's mouth crept into a smile. "I've got an idea."

CHAPTER 9

"My dad's a fisherman," Kai explained as he led Maya into the basement of his house. "It's not his full-time job or anything, but he heads out pretty much every day." He led them to a cooler and opened it, revealing a bunch of whole, big fish stacked on top of one another. "We eat some of it, but he sells the majority to local restaurants for some extra cash." He turned toward Maya. "If we throw these in the water, the shark will probably follow them. We can get it away from the sandbar to give you a better shot at Paige."

Maya just stared at the fish for a moment, blinking slowly as she processed what Kai had just said. Truth be told, she didn't like the plan. It would be risky, and she would be the one taking most of the risk. Kai would just be chucking fish into the ocean while she was in the water with the shark. Still, with the tide coming in and emergency services distracted by the shipwreck, Maya didn't have a better plan.

"It's worth a shot," she said. Kai nodded.

They each grabbed some fish from the cooler. They brought them out of the basement and threw them into the back of Kai's old beat-up pickup truck. No time to get a container to hold them.

"Let's go!" Maya practically shouted.

"We should get more." Kai was already headed back toward his basement.

"We don't have time to get more!"

He turned, clearly a little frustrated. "Do you want me to run out of fish while you're halfway back with Paige?" Maya just stood there. "No? Then let's go get some more, but let's do it quickly." He turned again and headed toward the basement.

Although she was antsy to get back to Ripper's Cove, Kai was making a lot of sense, so she followed him back to the cooler. Within a few minutes, they had twice the number of fish. Then they jumped in the truck and Kai peeled out of the driveway.

Kai was speeding down the road, but Maya could feel time slipping away from them.

"Come on! Go faster!"

"It's a thirty zone, and I'm already going close to forty," Kai replied. "If we get pulled over, it'll take us even longer to get there."

"If we get pulled over, we can tell the cop what's going on, and they can radio for help!"

Kai raised his eyebrows. It didn't seem like he'd thought of that. He pushed the car to forty-five, and the entire way to Ripper's Cove, Maya hoped she'd see flashing lights behind them.

But they didn't see another car on the entire journey there. Maya tried 911 several more times, but she still wasn't getting through.

Kai parked by the boardwalk, and they both got out. They whipped around to the back of the truck and started grabbing as many fish from the back as they could carry.

The smell was terrible. The fish were thawing now that they were out in the heat, but that would probably make them more appetizing to the shark.

Maya ran down to the water, tripping a little bit over her feet, but managing to stay upright. She peered out over the waves. Paige was still out there, lying motionless on the sandbar exactly where Maya had left her. The sandbar appeared to have shrunk in the time it took Maya to return. She hoped it was just her imagination. If the tide really was coming in already, they wouldn't have much time at all.

"We need to take the fish farther away!" Kai shouted when he saw where she was standing, still holding the fish. "We need the shark to be lured away." He was running with his load of fish to the other end of Ripper's Cove, as far from Paige as he could get. Maya followed, and they dropped the fish in a big slimy pile on the other end of the cove.

"Come on," he said. "Let's get the rest from the truck."

Maya went back for the second load, and when all the fish were piled up on the rocks next to Kai, she ran to the other end of the cove.

There was practically no sign there had even been a storm that day. The sun was peeking out through a few scattered clouds, but it was low in the sky. Maya knew that by the time it went down, the tide would be in, and the sandbar would be underwater. She guessed that they had about forty-five minutes to bring Paige back. If they didn't manage that, the sea or the shark would get her.

"Do you see it?" Kai shouted from the other end of the cove. Maya had to strain to hear him across the huge distance between them.

Maya scanned the water. There was no

sign of the shark's dorsal fin, but she didn't want to get in unless she was positive the predator had moved on.

"No," she shouted back. "But it was here not long ago!"

Kai may have nodded, but it was too hard to tell from this distance.

Maya waited, looking intently at the water. Once again, she felt paralyzed and useless. Her friend wasn't that far, but Maya didn't dare start toward her until she knew where the shark was. For now, all she could do was wait.

"I'm throwing one!" Kai yelled.

Using a pocket knife, Kai opened the belly of the fish. Then he threw it in a wide arc, as far into the ocean as he could. The splash made Maya flinch.

More waiting. The dead fish was in the water, but there was no way to know if the shark was going to take the bait. Until Maya saw something.

Like a razor blade cutting its way out of the water, the shark's dorsal fin appeared maybe thirty feet out from where Maya was standing. It was headed toward the dead fish.

"It's here!" she shouted and pointed at the fin cutting its way through the waves.

Kai didn't say anything, but she saw him slice open another fish and throw it into the water. The fin started moving a little faster, and Maya knew it was chasing the smell of fish guts.

She waited until the shark was halfway between her and Kai before grabbing her board, racing into the water, and gently paddling toward the sandbar. She wanted so badly to go fast. Even in the brief time they'd waited for the shark to appear, the sandbar had definitely shrunk. They had a half hour at best, but Maya knew that sharks were attracted to kicking and splashing. If she paddled as hard as she could, she might attract the shark to her instead of their fish bait.

She dove under the waves as they came in but tried to keep her motion fluid and calm.

Each time she popped her head back out of the water, she half expected the shark to be right next to her.

Maya heard another splash—Kai throwing another fish into the water. It was best that he did so regularly, keeping the shark distracted long enough for Maya to get Paige on her board and to the shore.

Maya was halfway there. She could see Paige clearly now. More important, she could see that one of Paige's arms looked like it was touching the water. The sandbar was shrinking fast. Time was running out.

Once again, Maya felt the strong urge to go faster, paddle as hard as she could to save her friend. *That would make things worse*, she reminded herself. *Slow and steady. Slow and steady.*

She felt her foot hit the ground. She was close enough to the sandbar to run up onto it. She got off her board just as she heard another fish hitting the water.

"Paige!" she shouted. "Paige, wake up!"

Paige didn't move, and for a second, Maya

thought the worst. She put a hand near Paige's mouth and felt the slightest exhale. Maya took a deep, relieved breath and prepared to do something she knew Paige wouldn't like.

She laid her friend's board on the sand next to her and grabbed Paige by the shoulders. "Sorry about this," she said. She pulled Paige onto the board in one quick motion.

The movement in her broken leg must have been unbearable because Paige woke up screaming. "Why?" Paige shouted at Maya through tears.

"We have to get you to shore! I'm sorry, but we have to do it now! The tide is coming in, and we don't have long before you'll be underwater."

Paige looked around, obviously a little dazed from passing out. She didn't seem to recognize the sandbar. Maya considered telling her about the shark, but it was probably best not to panic her friend any further. She was already in pain.

"Hold on to your board with one hand and

my leg with the other. I'm going to guide you to shore, okay?"

Paige nodded, and Maya gripped the edge of Paige's board and dragged it into the water. Paige winced, but she seemed relatively okay.

"We're going to go nice and slow, okay?" Maya said, trying to use her most reassuring voice even though she didn't think she'd ever been this nervous. "I'll be right in front of you, so let me know if there's a problem. I'll take care of it."

Paige nodded again. "Okay," she said.

Maya heard another splash in the distance.

Good, she thought. *Kai's still keeping the shark far away from us.*

Maya got positioned on her board and stuck out her leg for Paige to grab. Once she was sure her friend had a good grip, Maya began paddling. In the wake of the storm, the waves had calmed dramatically. They weren't even big enough to surf on at this point. Maya was thankful. She didn't know if Paige would be able to hold on all the way to shore if she had to fight the waves.

Maya continued paddling, slow and steady. The last thing she wanted to do was try to hurry and risk making Paige's broken leg worse. Or get the shark's attention.

They'd only made it about thirty or forty feet from the sandbar when Maya heard panicked shouting. It was Kai. He was running along the beach screaming, "Go! Go! Go!" at the top of his lungs.

CHAPTER 10

"Is that Kai?" Paige asked groggily from her board, pivoting her head to look at the shore.

"Yeah," Maya replied. Her heart was racing in her chest, but she was trying to remain calm. "He's . . . helping."

"Helping what?" Paige asked skeptically. "He's not even in the water."

Maya stared a little harder. Kai didn't have a fish in his hand. He was waving his arms and frantically pointing at the water while shouting something that Maya couldn't understand because he was much too far away.

But Maya knew exactly what he was trying

to say. He was out of fish, and the shark was coming their way.

"Paige, listen," Maya said over her shoulder, still trying to remain as calm as possible. "We have to go faster. A lot faster."

"Why?" Paige replied. "And what's Kai doing here? Doesn't he have a competition or something to—"

"There's a shark, Paige." She couldn't waste any more time, and this was no time for debate.

"Hold on to my leg." Maya started paddling faster. She heard Paige inhale sharply. The sudden jolt of motion must have jostled her leg. "We'll be on shore before you know it." Maya said, not sure if she was trying to convince herself or Paige.

Maya was scanning the water while she paddled. If she had any luck at all, she'd see the fin before the shark saw her. She was paddling at full strength, but still not going as fast as usual. Dragging her friend behind her was like having an anchor latched to her ankle. Every time the current brushed them sideways, Maya had to correct their path.

Kai was standing on the shore, right where Maya and Paige would make landfall. He was leaning forward, clearly watching the water for any motion—any sign of the bull shark that threatened them.

They were over halfway to the shore, and for a second, Maya thought everything would be okay. Maybe the shark had gotten its fill from all the fish and had swum back out to sea, leaving them alone. They'd make it safely to shore, Kai could drive Paige to the hospital, and this whole incident could become a distant memory.

"Look out!" Kai's voice shot across the water.

Maya turned just in time to see the dorsal fin only a few feet from Paige's board. It bumped into the surfboard, dumping Paige into the water. Her hand slipped off Maya's ankle, and she sank.

In an instant, Maya rolled off her own board and began the frantic search for her friend. She spotted Paige just below her, using her hands to propel herself upward toward the surface.

As soon as Paige popped up Maya started yelling. "Get on the board! Get on the board!"

Paige wrapped her hands around her own board and tried to pull herself up, but she winced in pain and looked at Maya with desperation on her face.

Maya quickly looked around her. There was no sign of the fin, but the shark had to be close, and the gash on Paige's leg had probably reopened in the water, pumping out blood. The fish was sure to circle around.

"This is going to hurt," Maya said. Paige nodded.

Maya dove under the water. She grabbed her friend's legs—one of them felt like it had two knees. Then Maya lifted the legs up over her head and in a quick motion, came out of the water and tossed the legs onto the board.

Paige was screaming and crying loudly. It hurt Maya to hear, but it had to be done.

There was no time for Maya to get on her own board. Besides, the ankle leash would make sure it trailed behind her. She got behind Paige and started pushing, kicking her legs as fast as she could, holding onto the back of the board to keep herself afloat. She was trying to be a human motor, propelling her friend forward.

Kai was in the shallow, waist-high water. *He's probably afraid to go in any farther*, Maya thought. But he had his arms stretched out, ready to take Paige's hands when they got close enough. He'd pull her into shore if Maya could just get her close enough.

"It's coming back!" he shouted.

Maya turned to her right. Sure enough, the dorsal fin was poking out of the water and headed straight for her. All of her kicking and flailing was attracting its attention.

The shark closed in just as a wave was rolling them toward the shore. Maya gave Paige's board a quick shove forward, then quickly repositioned and tried to push herself backward.

It worked. The shark swam right between them, but Maya spotted the top part of its jaw sticking out of the water, reaching for the prey that had been there just a moment ago. *Reaching for us*, Maya thought with dread. It passed in a flash, and the dorsal fin sank into the water. Maya knew instantly that it was going to make another pass at them.

She started swimming as fast as she could. If the shark was going to attack again, she didn't have any time to spare. She reached Paige's board and gave it another strong shove forward. Between the push and Paige paddling as hard as she could with her arms, Maya figured her friend would make it. Besides, the shark was probably fixated on her own flailing figure. Paige must have looked more like debris from the shark's perspective.

Maya started swimming again as hard and as fast as she could.

"On your left!" Kai warned.

The dorsal fin was poking out of the water again, and this time, Maya didn't trust herself to doge it.

She grabbed her board and held it above her head, using her legs to tread water. She tilted the board over one shoulder and prepared to strike at the shark at the last possible second.

Everything seemed to slow down, like the world had been put into slow motion. Just as the shark's head came lunging forward, Maya swung the board. She hit the shark across its snout and the shark recoiled from her, momentarily stunned. But she could tell by the look in its eyes that the shark wasn't done with her yet. It ducked down below the water and circled back around her for another strike. This time Maya was less prepared. She swung her board awkwardly, and it lodged in the shark's open jaws.

The shark clamped down on the board and ripped it straight out of Maya's hands.

Take off the ankle leash! Maya thought in a panic.

Before the shark had time to pull her away with the board, Maya ducked her head underwater and undid the strap. No sooner had she done it than the rubber leash was tugged out of her hands by the shark.

Popping her head out of the water, she saw

Kai dragging the surfboard, with Paige still on it, up onto the shore. She breathed a sigh of relief and stared swimming again.

The shark didn't make another pass at her, but Maya didn't feel truly safe until she was completely out of the water on the dry, jagged rocks of Ripper's Cove.

CHAPTER 11

Once she made it to shore, Maya rested
her pounding head in her hands, the world
spinning once more. Even though the rocks
were poking her in the back, she lay on the
beach. Maya was grateful that both she and
Paige had made it to dry land alive and mostly
in one piece. Her only regret was that she'd
lost a perfectly good surfboard in the process.
Still, she would trade a surfboard for her life
and the life of her friend any day.

"That was pretty impressive," Kai said. "I've
never seen anyone take on a bull shark before."

"Thanks," Maya said flatly, staring at the
spinning sky.

"If it's not too much trouble," Paige said. "I'd like to get to the hospital."

"Right." Maya tried to jump up, but only managed to get to a seated position before turning around and throwing up.

"Should I try again to get an ambulance?" Kai asked, looking with concern at both Paige and Maya.

Paige turned to her friend. "You clearly need to see a doctor too."

"I'll be fine," Maya replied in a soft voice. "But I think if you could drive us to the hospital now, that would be good, Kai."

Kai helped Paige up. By putting most of her weight on Kai, Paige was able to hop on one foot.

Maya tried to stand again, but the world went fuzzy as soon as she lifted her head.

"Just lie down, and I'll come back for you once Paige is in my car," Kai said.

Maya didn't need to be told twice. She took a deep breath and closed her eyes.

"You need to stay awake," Kai said sharply.

Maya groaned but opened her eyes.

Once he got Maya and Paige safely in his truck, Kai drove all three of them to the hospital a few miles away. Paige used his phone to call her dad and Maya's parents and tell them what had happened.

Maya tried to focus on her knees rather than the world flashing by her outside. Kai and Paige were chatting more casually than Maya would have thought possible given what they'd just been through, but Maya didn't join in on the conversation. She shut her eyes to keep the nausea at bay. Her head throbbed with every bump they went over. Maya was so tired. All she wanted to do was sleep.

A sudden pain jolted Maya awake. Kai was yelling her name and smacking her arm to try and get her to wake up.

Maya groaned and blinked a few times. Flashing lights to her right told her they were almost to the hospital. Her eyes fluttered shut again and Kai's yells drifted farther and farther away.

* * *

Maya woke up in a dark room to a whispered conversation floating off to her left. She recognized her parents' voices but not the others.

Maya looked around at the closed curtain hanging around her hospital bed. She thought about reaching out for the curtain, but her muscles ached and even lifting her arm felt like an impossible task. So instead she said in a croaky voice, "Hello?" Her word came out so soft even she could barely hear it. She cleared her throat and tried again, louder this time.

The curtain opened a crack and a smiling doctor looked in at her. "Hello, Maya. How are you feeling?"

Maya shrugged. "Like I was hit by a bus."

The doctor gave a soft chuckle. "Well, that doesn't seem surprising given what you've been through. Can you tell me what day it is?"

CHAPTER 12

Maya was diagnosed with a concussion and told she had to stay overnight for observation. By the next morning, Maya was out of her mind with boredom. Her parents were sitting in the dark hospital room with her, but seemed to be taking the doctor's "minimal talking" suggestion to heart. Maya also wasn't allowed to listen to music, watch television, read, or focus on anything for an extended period of time. She had started to look forward to the regular check-ins from doctors and hospital staff just for something to do.

Maya sighed and rolled over in her bed. If she craned her neck slightly, she could see a sliver of the doorway from where she was lying.

After a while of watching visitors and doctors make their down the hallway, a large white cast and the wheels of a wheelchair came into view. Paige knocked on the doorway gently and then let herself in.

Maya's parents greeted Paige and left to go find some coffee.

Maya smiled and sat up. "Hey," she said. She hadn't realized that her friend was still in the hospital. "Are you trapped here too?"

"For a little while longer," Paige smiled at her. "They just wanted to make sure there wasn't an infection, but they're releasing me at noon. My dad's at home getting the living room ready. Since I can't use stairs for a while, I'll basically be living there for the next few months."

"Ah, that makes sense," Maya said as Paige wheeled herself alongside Maya's bed. "So you'll be sleeping on a couch, and I'll be trapped in dark rooms. What an exciting pair we make."

Paige looked over at her, concern in her eyes. "Sorry about your concussion. I hadn't realized you were hurt when you came back out to the sandbar to get me."

"There's no way I was leaving you out there," Maya shrugged. "Sorry about your leg."

"It'll heal just like your head. Then we'll be able to hit the waves again." She chuckled a little. "At least neither of us got eaten by the shark, right?"

Maya let out a puff of laughter. "True. Very true."

There was another soft knock on the doorframe, and Maya turned to see Kai standing there holding a surfboard under one arm and a plastic to-go container under the other.

"Mind if I come in?" he asked. Paige waved him in. Kai stepped forward, putting the container on the bedside table between Paige and Maya. "I was in here to get my appendix out a year ago. The food's terrible, so I brought you some breakfast."

Paige popped the top. "Hey! Bacon!"

"And an omelet," he smiled.

Paige immediately started in on the food, but Maya still wasn't very hungry.

Kai smiled at Paige's enthusiasm. Then, turning to face Maya he said, "I brought you this." He laid the board out next to her on the bed. "I won it at a competition, but I figured you deserve it more."

Maya looked at the board. "You don't have to give this to me."

"Yeah," he replied. "I kind of do. If I had just let you surf with us, this wouldn't have happened. That's not a mistake I'll repeat." He put his hand over his heart. "Promise. I told some of the others what happened. They thought it was awesome, and uhh, well, they're gonna call you Shark, but you can surf with us any time."

"They're going to call me Shark?" Maya raised an eyebrow.

"Yeah." He pointed to the board. "I was up late last night, so I painted that."

Maya flipped it over to see a painting of a cartoon bull shark with a surfboard between its jaws.

Maya couldn't help but laugh. "I love it."

"Well," Paige said, chewing on a strip of bacon. "I vote we never go to Ripper's Cove again. All in favor say 'aye.'"

"Aye," Maya said.

About the Author

R. T. Martin lives in St. Paul, Minnesota. When he is not drinking coffee or writing, he is busy thinking about drinking coffee and writing. He is left-handed and has made exactly one good tiramisu.

TO THE LIMIT

OFF ROAD

ON EDGE

RIPTIDE

WHITEOUT

CHECK OUT ALL THE TITLES IN THE
TO THE LIMIT SERIES

DAY OF DISASTER

AFTERSHOCK
Vanessa Acton

BACKFIRE
Vanessa Acton

BLACK BLIZZARD
Kristin F. Johnson

DEEP FREEZE
Kristin F. Johnson

VORTEX
Vanessa Acton

WALL OF WATER
Kristin F. Johnson

Would you survive?